SHADOWED DESIRES

DIDI M DARLING

Book Cover by Kiel Gettler

ISBN 978-1-7388356-6-9 (Paperback)

ISBN 978-1-7388356-7-6 (Ebook)

Stay Awkward Publishing

 Created with Vellum

CONTENT WARNING

This novella may not be for you if you are not open to a woman who is unafraid to explore and celebrate her sexuality. She enjoys the pleasure of men and women, and appreciates a battery-operated option as well.

This novella contains language so nasty you will want to wash your mouth out with soap.

You may become sexually attracted to your shadow, or others. Read this book in bright lighting.

An unrealistic perfect book boyfriend may have been created. I'm sorry. No, I'm not talking about Eric.

Contains unwanted sexual advances.

Suicide and Murder are briefly mentioned.

CONTENTS

Everyone loves a Shadow Daddy, but talk to me when you have fucked a shadow.

CHAPTER ONE

"Let me taste you. Just once."

"I said no."

Evelyn's boss was persistent. One of her bosses. His older brother owned the company, and Brock was a dangerous pity hire. Brock had been making escalated advancements toward her for the last few weeks. Standing at six-foot-two, with dark hair, a strong jawline, and a muscular build that showed he definitely didn't skip leg day, he was, by far, the most attractive man in their office, if not in the entire skyrise. He was also the worst player. Very few people have shown concern that he abused his position to sleep around, while the majority of women believed it was a privilege just to be hit on by him. There was a rumour that he was trying to sleep with every woman in the building, available or married. A rumour he had never admitted to, or denied.

Evelyn wasn't interested in being a statistic.

To Brock's credit, he had been trying to sleep with her for the past two years. He had asked her out on her first day as IT manager, but she politely declined. She didn't want to go out with the first person who asked, wanting to get a feel for the office environment and her coworkers before she started dating at work.

She wasn't opposed to dating someone from the office, but she had learned the hard way that people aren't always who they present themselves to be. She had to leave her last job after she got involved with a woman who claimed to be single and then had to deal with the woman's angry husband when their affair was discovered. Most men fantasize about finding their wife's face buried in the pussy of another woman, but he freaked out and later showed up to their work and destroyed a lot of property instead.

Evelyn was fixing the copier when Brock snuck behind her. She wouldn't put it past him to have created the massive paper jam just to get her alone in the small closet-like room where the copier and supplies were kept. He had come up behind her and pressed his pelvis into her ass before he whispered his request into her ear.

She should have known that saying no wasn't going to be enough.

"Why are you fighting this?" he asked, as he pressed harder into her. Her back stiffened when she could feel his hard cock rubbing against her. He noticed. "This is all you Evie. This is what you do to me," he said as he started to grind into her.

Fuck, it's been a while, she thought to herself.

She hadn't slept with anyone in months. His cock, which felt impressively vast, was so tempting.

Instead, she elbowed him in the ribs to escape his advances.

"You need to stop," she said, barely above a whisper. She was worried someone would walk by and misinterpret the situation. She couldn't have anyone think she would partake in anything like this at work.

At least, not with the door opened.

"Evelyn, you are so beautiful. This isn't about some stupid

numbers game, not with you. If I had you, I wouldn't need to fuck anyone else," he declared.

She was beautiful. Recently turning twenty-nine (for the third time), she stood at 5'6, with natural dark auburn hair that fell to her shoulder blades, usually worn down in loose curls. Her skin was fair, with splashes of freckles sporadically across her body, and her nose. Natural full lips, a button nose and large blue eyes adorned her heart-shaped face. Her mid-sized figure carried an ass that was the envy of every woman who spent hours in the gym squatting, and her breasts were firm and appropriate for her size.

She was beautiful, and she knew it, so when some womanizer told her this, it didn't make her immediately want to drop her panties.

"But you have fucked like half the women in this building. That's a little gross, Brock."

"Babe, if you are worried about whether I'm clean, I just got tested. We have a clean bill of health," he said, as he grabbed his cock over his pants and shook it.

He did not just refer to him and his cock as "we."

Evelyn rolled her eyes and chuckled at the absurdity. Brock saw it as a change of heart. He stepped closer to her and tugged at the knee of her ankle-length skirt.

"I don't even want you to touch me. This is all for you. Let me make you feel good," he said, walking her backwards into the solid side of a supply shelf. He stepped into her, and had both hands on her skirt, slowly bunching up the fabric in his fingers. He had her skirt just above her knees when he leaned in and rubbed his nose up her neck before he whispered in her ear, "I just know you are going to taste amazing. I'm going to fuck you so hard with my tongue, it's going to make my cock jealous. I'm going to make you come so many times, you'll be begging to ride my face every night. Lucky for you, I'm a generous man."

Jesus

She was tempted. She was a breath away from lifting her skirt herself and shoving it over his head to make him make good on all his promises. She wanted this, needed this.

He took her silence as consent and dropped to his knees. He slowly brought her skirt up to the top of her thighs and moaned softly when he saw her black-laced panties were already wet with anticipation.

"I knew you were a naughty girl," his husky voice said as he sat back on his heels admiring her.

It was this stalled moment of arrogance and admiration that snapped Evelyn out of her aroused stupor and gave her a moment of clarity. If Brock had just gone straight to licking her pussy instead of admiring it as a trophy or conquest won, she would have succumbed to the sensation and would have lost all conscious thought and control.

But he hesitated.

Evelyn shoved Brock's head back, making him lose balance and fall over. She straightened her skirt and composed herself.

"Give it up Brock. It's never going to happen," she stated, walking over him to get to the still-opened door.

No matter how great your cock is rumoured to be, she thought with a sigh as she looked back at him once more before leaving.

She locked herself in her office for the remainder of the day, afraid she wouldn't be able to deny herself again if Brock decided that was merely foreplay.

CHAPTER TWO

When Evelyn got home that night, she took a cold shower.

She needed to. That encounter with Brock, though annoying, was hot. She spent the rest of the afternoon with her thighs pressed together under her desk and had to keep her hands busy by answering e-mails, to stop herself from slipping a hand under her skirt to relieve her aching, throbbing clit, or from tweaking her nipples, which stayed pebbled all day from her constant state of arousal.

The shower barely brought her relief. As she washed herself, she got lost in the feel of her hands soaping up her ample breasts, gliding down her stomach, her fingers teasing her hungry cunt.

"No!" she said aloud. "I refuse to finger myself thinking about that jerk," she said tearing her fingers away. "Even though it would have been so fucking hot to have him kneeling before me, eating me out, door open, with reception just on the other side of the wall," she admitted, fingers sliding back down.

She stopped herself again and then turned the water to the coldest setting she could handle to finish her shower. The bitter cold acted as penance for even entertaining the thought of letting Brock do unspeakable, dirty things to her.

To avoid another act of atonement, she decided that she absolutely could not touch herself for the remainder of the night. Even if she thought about her morally grey vampire book boyfriend, or the cute blonde with the perky tits who lived on the third floor of her apartment building while she played with her toys, she was afraid her mind would drift off to choking on Brock's huge veiny throbbing cock.

Michelle from HR had given Evelyn a meticulously detailed description of his dick after she sucked him off during last year's Christmas party. Susan, from accounting confirmed those details after she let him bend her over his desk after hours when everyone had left for the night. Greg, head of maintenance, also couldn't get over the size of Brock's dick after watching Brock bend Susan over the desk while polishing the floor.

She made her lunch for tomorrow, watched a stupid comedy with zero sex appeal on one of her prescribed streaming channels, and then went to bed.

Evelyn had been asleep for a few hours when she was jolted awake by a vibrating noise. A continuous buzzing assaulted the quiet of the night. She sat up, her heart racing so fast, that she was afraid it would soon cease to beat at all in a moment.

"Hello? Who's there?" she asked aloud, sounding braver than she felt. Before she went to bed, Evelyn had triple-checked all four locks on her apartment door. She lived on the tenth floor of the building, so she wasn't sure how someone could have gotten into her apartment. Some women fantasize about the idea of an intruder breaking in and ravishing them, but she would rather not be sexually assaulted by some stranger with their knife or gun.

Hard limit.

The noise persisted. A strange rattling noise accompanied the buzzing.

As her drowsiness started to lift, she realized the sound was coming from the right side of her room. Shaking, she slowly scooted over to the other side of her queen-sized bed to investigate the unnerving activity.

It was coming from her nightstand.

With a shaky hand, she reached out and whipped the top drawer open, then threw herself to the other side of the bed, grabbing a pillow as a means of protection. When nothing flew out to murder her, she crawled back over and peeked into the drawer.

"Are you fucking kidding me?" she laughed with relief.

It was her vibrator. Her favourite suctioning vibrator was rattling around her drawer, set at full vibration.

"How did that even get turned on?" she asked. It was the dead of night, she hadn't used it that day, and there was nothing in the drawer that could have turned it on.

She grabbed it and turned it off, inspecting it to see how it could have powered on, and then for any damage. This vibrator had been her lifeline to sanity since her internet dating had recently dried up. There were only so many "men holding fish in profile pics" she could date, and the ones she did, were selfish fucks, who were more focused on trying to stick their dick in her ass, than worrying about if she came.

"Wait..." Evelyn paled and dropped the toy in her lap. "How...?"

She froze in fear. She kept all her toys in her nightstand on the left side of the bed, where she slept. She had never put any of her vibrators, wands, suction toys, handcuffs, nipple clamps, strap-ons, dildos, vibrating panties, cock rings, anal beads, butt plugs, ball gags, tassel whips, or feather ticklers in the right-side nightstand. She didn't even put her extra lube in it. So how did it end up in there?

"Someone's been in here," she whispered, eyes wide in fear.

She tried to listen for footsteps, heavy breathing, or the constant slap of a perv jerking himself off hiding in a dark corner, but she couldn't hear anything over the blood pounding in her ears. When the roaring in her ears finally subsided, her heart rate calming down with time, she was able to have a proper look around her room. Her eyes had fully adjusted to the dark. Everything looked in order in her room. She switched the light on her left-side nightstand, got up, and did a quick, but thorough tour of her apartment, checking every possible spot a person could be hiding.

"This is stupid, you are being stupid!" she scolded herself on her walk back to the bedroom. "I probably put it in there when I was drunk or something," she tried to convince herself.

On the way back to her room, she backtracked to the kitchen and switched on the light above the stove. Some nights she needed to sleep with this light on if her claustrophobia flared up. Sometimes she couldn't handle it when it was too dark. Tonight, she needed the extra comfort.

She returned her vibrator to its rightful place, settled back into bed, and turned the light off. When she was getting herself into her preferred sleeping position, face down, ass up, she remembered that she left the drawer opened on the other nightstand. She couldn't sleep with closets and drawers opened.

Annoyed and tired, she threw the blankets off of her and crawled over to close it. As she reached for the drawer, a black hand reached for it at the same time.

CHAPTER THREE

S he pulled her hand back and screamed.

The hand pulled back at the same time.

A nervous laugh escaped her lips.

"It's just your fucking shadow, you stupid bitch," she said feeling foolish. But when she started to turn around to crawl back to the other side, she saw her shadow again, behind her, on the wall where her headboard sits. The hand she saw came from the other wall and had reached out towards her.

She froze.

There was someone or *something* in the room.

Move, run, do something! Her mind was pleading with her to get out of there, but her fear kept her rooted in place. Frozen on all fours, ass presented to her intruder.

She was able to turn her head and glance over her shoulder. A tall silhouette of a person stood beside the bed.

Tears started to fall as her eyes grew wide in terror, afraid to blink and miss any sudden movement. She still couldn't move, but the figure didn't as well, as if they were staring back at her. Studying her as she watched them. It didn't have eyes, but she swore she could feel their eyes boring into her own, and then sweeping across her body, landing on her exposed ass.

That helped her move.

She flipped onto her back and crab-walked to the far side of the bed, grabbing a pillow to cover her body. She had gone to bed in her usual tank top and panties, so she felt exposed. She fought to breathe, taking shallow breaths when her body allowed it. Her body betrayed her once more and ignored her silent pleas to run out of her apartment.

As they continued to stare at each other, or she assumed it was staring, she realized that it wasn't exactly a silhouette. It was translucent, like a shadow. A three-dimensional shadow.

A 3D shadow?

She watched it tilt its head as if in thought, terrified at what conclusion it was coming to.

"What...what do you want?" she managed to say. Her voice sounded foreign and small.

It didn't answer, but how could it? It had no mouth.

The being turned towards her shadow, huddled on the wall beside her. It looked taken by surprise, as if it was just noticing her shadow for the first time. It ran a hand through its shadowed hair, and Evelyn caught the hint of a bicep. It started to walk towards her shadow, positioned above the other side of the bed on the wall.

Evelyn determined the being was male. If the height and muscular build didn't give it away, it was in the way he walked. He had an arrogance to his swagger. She was getting "I have a big dick and you would be lucky to get to suck it," energy.

Can a shadow be a douchebag?

When he reached her shadow, he extended his arm. Evelyn braced herself, worried she would be able to feel whatever he did to it. It didn't make sense, but neither did this entire situation.

Was he trying to hurt it, and by extension, hurt her?

What if he murdered her shadow?

Would she die too? Or can she live without it? If she could, would she feel like a piece of herself would always be missing?

She knew she should move to save her shadow. If she ran, it would have to follow. Instead, she sat there, mouth open, staring in awe to see what he wanted. To see what would happen. She cursed herself. She had no fight or flight, just dumbstruck idiocracy.

He reached for her shadow's face, his fingers tracing the outline. He brought his other hand up to do the same. Her shadow didn't respond, because Evelyn didn't respond.

He leaned in and pressed his head to the head of her shadow.

A shadow kiss.

It looked so sweet and tender. She couldn't remember the last time anyone had kissed her like that. Lately, it had been all fast-paced tongue and teeth. Men rushed the kissing part, more interested in shoving their dick in her mouth. Even the last few women she fooled around with cared more about her other lips.

Was she jealous of her shadow?

Her shadow responded, bringing her hands up to grab his wrists, leaning into him, deepening the kiss.

"Wait, what the fuck..." Evelyn whispered, still huddled on the other side of the bed, holding a pillow against her. She watched in horror as her shadow moved independently, making out with the strange being.

His kiss brought her to life.

"Leave her alone!" she yelled at him.

"Fight back! You don't have to take this!" she pleaded with her shadow.

He broke their kiss, grabbed her arms and pulled her off the wall. Evelyn's shadow was now standing beside the strange trespasser, now a 3D being. He pulled her into his arms, kissing her deeply once again.

"Wake the fuck up, Evelyn. This is just a dream...you need to wake up!"

He started to get rougher with her shadow, grabbing her ass, and tugging at her hair at the base of her neck. He spun her around and tightly held her to his chest, grinding himself into her ass.

"Stop! You can't do that to her! Leave her alone!" Evelyn cried out. She started sobbing as she watched this assault on her shadow.

Except, she liked it. As he ground into her ass, her shadow grabbed his hands, placing them on her breasts, encouraging him to pinch her nipples, while she rubbed her ass against him.

"Seriously?" Evelyn asked. "This isn't happening."

But it was, and she watched with morbid fascination.

While one hand continued squeezing and pinching her breasts, the other slipped down, teasing her pussy.

Can a shadow even get wet? She thought.

It had become a three-dimensional being, like him, but besides outlines of body parts, they had no distinct definition. His hand went in between her legs, but she couldn't see his fingers brushing lips, or rubbing her clit, yet, she knew that was precisely what was happening. Like now, she knew he had at least two fingers pounding her cunt, while another finger teased her asshole.

My shadow is a dirty girl, she thought, as she watched the scene unfold.

She couldn't feel what her shadow experienced, but it was almost like she had a sixth sense of knowing what was being done to her.

Her shadow broke free, turned around and dropped to her

knees. Evelyn watched as his shadow cock grew and extended from his body.

Mr. Shadow had a massive, girthy cock.

Her shadow greedily grabbed it with both hands and shoved it into her mouth. Her head moved up and down his translucent shaft, taking him down to the base. Unlike her, her shadow didn't have a gag reflex.

Lucky bitch.

While she worked his cock with her mouth, he grabbed her head, tangling his fingers into her wispy hair, encouraging the momentum she had started. He watched her intently, throwing his head back in pleasure every few moments, losing himself to the sensation. After an impressive length of time, his grip tightened and he stilled her head while he was fully buried in her mouth and spilled down her throat.

Do shadows come? Did he just pour more shadow down her throat? How the fuck does this even work? Evelyn thought.

She was still scared. Terror kept her still and watching, but she found that even if she could leave right now, a part of her wanted to stay and watch. It was like driving past a car accident. Inquisitiveness had won.

He untangled his fingers from her hair, placed a hand under her chin, and guided her to a standing position. He lowered his head, took her mouth, and wrapped her arms around his neck. As he kissed her hard and deep, he grabbed the back of her thighs, lifted her, spun her around and threw her onto the foot of the bed.

Evelyn impossibly felt the mattress shift.

He positioned her shadow at the edge of the bed, knelt in front of her, placed her legs on his shoulders and started eating her out.

Within seconds, her back was arched and she was writhing from what Evelyn assumed was intense pleasure. He held her down at the hips, as he continued his assault on her cunt. Licking, sucking, and biting, while he fucked her with his fingers. Her shadow made no sound, but if she could, Evelyn knew she would be screaming obscenities.

After what looked like three quick orgasms, he stood up and dropped his massive shadowy dick onto her pussy, rubbing her with it, bringing her to another climax before he slammed himself into her cunt to the hilt. He fucked her relentlessly, his intensity only changing to faster thrusts. He grabbed her legs, and held them straight to his body, her heels facing the ceiling, as he penetrated her at a deeper level.

Fuck, this guy has stamina, Evelyn thought as she watched in awe as he never missed a stride, or showed any fatigue. Most guys she had been with were one-and-done. She either sucked them off, and they passed out from exhaustion, or they blew their load with a quick fuck, and then passed out from exhaustion.

He waited until her shadow came once more before he climaxed with her. Evelyn made a note that he had come inside her.

Apparently, they aren't worried about a little shadow surprise, she thought and snorted out loud at the ridiculousness of it all.

When they were finished, he grabbed her shadow's hands, helping her stand. Hand-in-hand, he walked her back to the wall, kissed her on the knuckle, and assisted her as she stepped back into the wall, returning to mirror Evelyn's curdled-up position.

Fear spiked through Evelyn again, as he turned his attention to her. But he just stood there, staring at her once more. She wanted to scream at him to stay away, to leave her alone, but she found herself unable to move again, mute and struggling with her breathing. He gave her a slight bow, turned around and then took a step forward and melted into the darkness.

CHAPTER FOUR

"Good morning, beautiful."

"You don't get the privilege of talking to me right now, or for the unforeseeable future, unless it is work-related," Evelyn said sternly to Brock.

It was the next morning. The workday hadn't even started yet, but Evelyn was pouring her third cup of coffee. Should she be speaking to her boss in such a way? Probably not, but being polite and professional was not getting her anywhere.

"Come on Evie, there's no hard feelings. You don't have to be like this," Brock said, inching closer to her.

Evelyn held out her arm, palm up, instructing him not to come any closer, took a sip of her coffee, and left without saying another word.

She couldn't deal with him right now. She blamed him for her unusual night. Brock came on to her. It was unwanted, but there was no denying that it was hot. She went to bed sexually frustrated and then dreamed the whole shadow fucking scenario, her dream manifesting her desires. The shadow represented Brock, and her shadow was her desire to fuck him.

At least, that was how she was justifying whatever that was.

The last thing she remembered was the mysterious figure disappearing into the night, and then she woke up twisted in her pillows and blankets when her alarm went off.

Just a dumb dream.

Still, she felt like she was up all night, and struggled to get through the day.

Later that afternoon, a few hours before quitting time, there was a knock at her door. It opened before she could answer and a man poked his head into her office.

"This doesn't look like a conference room, I'm so sorry to disturb..." he started, his words cutting off when he saw Evelyn sitting behind her desk.

"No," she chuckled. She stood up and walked towards the door. "You aren't even on the right side of the office," she clarified.

"So I'm not just a little lost..." he smirked.

"You're hopeless," she giggled, finishing his sentence.

"Hi, I'm Eric," he said, extending his hand in greeting.

"I know. Eric Stirling, hopefully, our soon-to-be most important client. I'm Evelyn," she said, shaking his hand.

She took advantage of the handshake to quickly look him over. She had seen plenty of pictures of Eric online, but they did him a disservice. He stood around 6'1, late thirties, athletic build and had dark hair with a bit of peppering on the sides. He wore an expensive suit, was clean-shaven, and had a woodsy-timber delicious smell.

Her panties were instantly wet.

"If you want to follow me, I can show you the way to the conference room," she said, breaking the handshake and walking past him out to the hall.

"That would be much appreciated. I'm already so late," he said.

"Mr. Stirling, you can be two hours late and everyone in there wouldn't bat an eye," she offered.

"Please, call me Eric," he said, with a panty-dropping smile. His teeth were so white and perfectly straight. She imagined her nipple caught between them, painfully being pulled and nibbled.

Get it together, Evelyn, she scolded herself. We can't lose this client.

"Anyway, Eric," she replied. "Everyone should already be waiting for you. We all know you are a very busy man, so your time won't be wasted."

"But you're not in there," he observed.

"No, I'm not needed."

"What is it you do here? You have your own office, so you must do more than be an escort."

"That would make me a pretty expensive escort," she laughed.

"Oh no!" Eric slapped his hand over his mouth, dragging it down. "I meant to say you must do more than escort people around. Show people around. That was a bad word choice. I would never...I'm so sorry!"

Evelyn burst out laughing.

"It's okay, really. I needed a laugh. No offence taken," she assured him.

"So...?" Eric asked, prompting her to continue.

"Oh, right. I'm the IT manager."

"So you run the entire place."

"Pretty much."

"If such a huge client were being hosted, shouldn't you be in there to make sure things run smoothly?"

"I set up everything ahead of time. Everything should work perfectly, unless there is some user error, of course. Then I would be called in."

"What if I need help with my laptop?"

"I can absolutely help with that."

"And can I request that you stay with me...by...stand by, stay in the room, in case I need assistance again? I have very little confidence in my tech ability," he said, with a cheeky smile.

"If that's what you want, we can make it happen. I aim to please. We aim...we, oh dear." She smacked her hand to her forehead, shaking her head in embarrassment.

"I think I'm going to like working with this company," he said, winking at her as they walked through the conference room doors.

Eric insisted that Evelyn sit beside him throughout the entire meeting. He pretended to need help connecting to the wifi network, which any toddler could manage, but she was more than happy to help. He annoyingly stayed professional during the meeting. His arm brushed hers once and didn't linger when it did.

What were you expecting? She thought to herself. *Footsies? Boob grazes? For him to grab your hand, shove it down his pants and have you jerk him off under the table while he discussed numbers with your bosses?*

There was something different about him. She could tell he was attracted to her, and she was sure she was giving him the same vibes. She checked his hand. No wedding ring, but that didn't mean he was available.

Or perhaps you found a fucking unicorn! Someone who cares to get to know you before they try to get their dick wet.

Naw...he probably has a fucking girlfriend. She sighed aloud, bringing his attention to her for a moment. She smiled at him, then pretended to check over her notes. *If they ever wanted a threesome though...*

When the meeting ended, Eric was getting his ass kissed by all the major bosses and the pitch team. Eric would decide in the following days whether he wanted to do business with their company. Evelyn didn't want to interrupt, so she quietly snuck out and headed to her office. It was time to go home anyway. She had almost forgotten how tired she was, Eric had been a nice distraction.

She checked her emails, saw there was nothing that needed her immediate attention, and started to pack her bag.

There was a soft knock at her door, then it opened a crack.

"Brock, I told you, it's never going to happen. That shit you pulled in the closet yesterday..."

"I'm not sure I met this *Brock* yet, but I'm instantly jealous of him, and suddenly want to hurt him, very badly," Eric said, voice laced with amusement but tinged with a hint of caution.

"Eric! I'm so sorry, I thought you were someone else," she gasped in embarrassment.

"I heard, some '*Brock*,'" he said, like it was a bad word, with a heavy emphasis on the "B." "What happened in the closet yesterday?"

"Nothing I can't handle," she assured him, her cheeks flushed with humility. He had not pieced together that her Brock was *the* Brock Collins who had just been kissing his ass for the past couple of hours. "What brings you back over to my end of the office?"

"Would you believe I got lost again?" he said with a teasing smile. "I could have sworn this was the exit."

Evelyn laughed. "Lucky for you, I was just on my way out. You can follow if you'd like."

She walked with him to the elevators. It arrived empty. He gestured for her to step in first, and then he followed, hitting the ground floor button.

"I have a confession," he started.

"Oh?" Evelyn asked, raising an inquisitive brow.

"I didn't get lost."

Evelyn gasped and clutched her hand to her chest, faking outrage.

"I know. I deceived you, I'm sorry," he chucked. "You just left the meeting without saying goodbye."

"I didn't want to get in the way or interrupt. You and the bosses were busy," she explained.

"Are you not a boss?"

"Yes, but not in *that* way. I run the IT department, but that isn't the business."

"Evelyn, if I work with your company, I expect to have my ass kissed by all the major players, so please, keep that in mind next time."

"Yes, Sir," she laughed.

"Shit," he said just under his breath. "Careful...," he warned in a teasing tone.

She gave him a sly smile back.

Well, this just got a little interesting...

The elevator doors opened. Eric cleared his throat and gestured for Evelyn to exit first. The lobby to the building was all glass, and she caught him checking out her ass in the window's reflection.

Maybe single after all?

"Anyway," he cleared his throat again before he continued. "I didn't want to leave without saying goodbye, and took a chance to see if you were still in your office."

"Well, I am glad you found me," Evelyn admitted, giving a friendly, but flirty smile.

"Me too. I wanted to talk to you about a coffee order."

Her heart sank. Her panties dried.

"Oh. Yes, of course. What can I have ready for you for your next visit?" she asked.

"What? Evelyn, no! Wow, I'm terrible at this. I wanted to know your order, so I can bring you a coffee and maybe steal you away for a break when I come back in two days for contract negotiations. Unless your boyfriend would mind?"

"He wouldn't," she said and watched a bit of hope die in his eyes. "I mean, because he doesn't exist. I don't know why I said that," she said nervously.

Fucking smooth, Evelyn!

Eric laughed. "So latte? Frappé? Iced coffee?"

"I like just regular coffee, two creams, one sugar. Nothing fancy," she replied.

"Great. Perfect. So, this is me," he said.

They arrived at his car, parked in front, in the VIP visitor parking spot. He drove a black McLaren Gt.

"Wow!" Evelyn exclaimed.

"Do you want a ride?"

"I'm tempted, but I have my car that I need to get home. Plus I need to buy deodorant on the way home, so..."

Why the fuck would I tell him that?

"Yes. Right. Well, thank you for all your help today. I guess I will see you on Thursday."

"Looking forward to it."

"Goodnight, Evelyn," Eric said, in a deep velvety voice, before opening his door, getting into his car and speeding off.

CHAPTER FIVE

"I need to buy deodorant on the way home," she said, in a mocking tone, for the hundredth time since being home. "Why? Why would you say that? He was interested and now he thinks you're a smelly freak! Why not just tell him you needed to buy a cleanser for your period cup? Or...or foot fungus cream or something! Fuck!"

Evelyn berated herself about this all night. After the meeting concluded, she wanted to rush home, take a shower, and then spend the evening playing with her toys, imagining what it would be like to fuck Eric. When he found her afterwards, she was pleased to have gathered even more material to use. There were definitely a few scenarios involving his sexy car she wanted to play out in her mind. On it, in it, half in, half out.

And his reaction to being called Sir.

But now, she was mortified.

She took another cold shower as punishment for her stupidity, not allowing herself any pleasure when she washed her breasts and genitals.

When Evelyn went through her bedtime routine, which

consisted of confirming all her locks were in place, windows secured, and closets closed, she hesitated when she reached the kitchen. Her strange dream came back to her, and she started to feel this weird sense of unease. She switched the light on over her stove. She didn't want to sleep in total darkness tonight.

After a half hour of scrolling through her socials, she managed to fall asleep.

Evelyn was jolted awake when she felt her mattress compress on the other side of the bed. She was facing the other way, and was too afraid to turn to see if she imagined the feeling, being in a state of half asleep, half awake, or if there was someone or *something* in her room. She brought her comforter up past her ears, willing for whatever was happening to go away. She held her breath and listened.

Silence. And all was still.

She slowly let out the breath she was holding. After a few minutes, she was confident she had half-dreamed the weird sensation. She lowered her comforter, took a sip of water, and rolled onto her back.

The dark figure was sitting at the foot of her bed.

Evelyn sat up, quickly scooting back until her ass hit the headboard. She pulled the blankets up to cover herself.

"No no no no...," she sobbed. "This isn't happening. This isn't real."

As she moved, she noticed that his attention was directed behind her. She glanced over her shoulder and saw her shadow.

"Did...did you just wake me up, to get to her?" Evelyn asked, voice shaking.

In answer, he stood and moved toward her shadow. He extended his hand, traced her face, and leaned in and kissed her.

Awestruck, Evelyn watched her shadow come to life, reach out from the wall, and grab the translucent intruder's outstretched hand. Once she was fully pulled away from the wall, they embraced and shared a deep kiss.

Wake up! Wake up wake up wake up! she implored her mind, but unlike the last time, she felt very awake, and much like the last night, it felt very real.

She pinched her arm. Hard. It hurt like a bitch.

Shit!

Although terrified, she wasn't paralyzed like before. She knew she could leave. She should leave.

There is a supernatural being stealing your shadow and using it to get off. For fucks sake, Move!

Can a shadow even give consent? What if the sex isn't enough to satisfy him this time? What if he was just toying with us, and this time he's out for blood?

She could run to the blonde on the third floor. They have been friendly enough that it wouldn't be too weird. There would be no doubt that she was distressed, showing up in her tank and underwear, so she would let Evelyn in.

Maybe she would comfort me in those huge perky tits until I felt safe enough to return to my apartment.

Fuck, why does being scared make me so horny.

She should have run, but she couldn't. Her morbid curiosity got the better of her, again. She would stay and watch.

At least someone is getting lucky, she thought, as she grabbed a pillow, hugging it tight.

The dark figure wasted no time and had moved to fondling, licking and sucking her shadow's breasts. Evelyn found her breasts had become heavy with want, her nipples pebbling with need.

She sighed.

The concupiscent trespasser heard her and stilled.

Shit shit shit. Stay quiet, you stupid idiot!

She was hoping that he had forgotten about her. That all his attention would stay on her shadow. Was she throwing her under the bus? Perhaps, but it's not like she wasn't enjoying it. She seemed all too eager to step out of the wall to get railed again.

He gave her shadow a quick kiss and held up his hand as if saying, "Just one moment." Then, to Evelyn's horror, he started to walk towards her. She expected him to walk around the bed, or crawl onto the bed to reach her, but he walked through it.

"What the...?" Evelyn let slip.

He was just sitting on her bed a few moments ago. His weight bearing down on her mattress woke her up, yet he was walking through it like it wasn't even there.

She held the pillow closer to her chest, willing it to be enough to protect her from him and whatever he had planned to do. When he was close enough to touch, she closed her eyes tight and held her breath, waiting for the oncoming assault. After a few seconds, when nothing happened, she dared to open her eyes and saw that he had walked past her. She found he had cleared her bed, and was standing beside her, next to her nightstand. She watched with horrified intrigue as he opened her nightstand, dug around, and pulled out the same suctioning vibrator she found misplaced the night before.

"It was you," Evelyn whispered. "You took it out."

To her utter astonishment, he nodded yes.

"Why?"

In response, he handed her the toy.

His fingers lightly grazed her palm, eliciting another gasp from her. It felt, both hot and cold and her hand tingled from the pleasant sensation. She held the vibrator and looked up at him.

"Um, thank you?" She wasn't sure what he wanted her to do.

He reached over, grabbed it once more, turned it on, and

placed it back in her hands. He gently pushed her hand towards her body.

"You...you want me to use it?"

He nodded yes.

"While watching you?"

He nodded.

"Watching you fuck her," she clarified, pointing her chin towards her shadow.

He nodded, enthusiastically, as if he was relieved she finally got with the program. His hand dropped down and grabbed his erect cock, and started to stroke it.

"This...this is what you wanted last night too?"

He nodded, as he started to walk through her bed, pumping his cock. When he passed her, he trailed his fingers softly along her face. The contact was brief, but it felt loving, safe, and instantly she knew he was not there to harm them.

The amorous invader cleared the bed and gathered her shadow into his arms, smashing his mouth down onto hers. His hands reached behind her, cupping and kneading her ass, before one slid down her thigh, scooping it up to hook her leg around his waist. He started kissing behind her ear, and down her neck, while his fingers teased her cunt from behind.

"Fuck, he knows what he's doing," Evelyn said to herself under her breath.

Her attention drifted from his actions to his physique. He was tall. She estimated he stood at least six-foot-three inches in height. His shoulders were broad, and his waist trimmed. If his see-through body had more definition, she knew he would have a six-pack and rippling back muscles. Her eyes were then drawn down and onto his rounded ass and thick thighs. Thighs that could easily support a cock ride from her mid-sized physique.

And what a cock it is...she thought.

Reluctantly, she tore her eyes away from his ass and found

his huge, throbbing smokey dick. It was rubbing against her shadow's abdomen as he kissed up and down her body while fingering her pussy.

The vibrator was still rumbling in Evelyn's hands as she stared at his body. He had her shadow's nipple in his mouth when he turned his head towards her. He released the nipple from his painful toothy grasp, (she imagined it like this anyway. Shadows probably don't have teeth, but they also don't barge into your home, steal your shadow, fuck it, and demand you touch yourself) and inclined his head towards her hands.

He was encouraging her to use it, and this time she obliged.

It was only when she positioned herself in a comfortable position, laying on the bed, and started to lower her vibrator to her pussy, did he turn his attention back to her shadow's plump, pebbled tits.

Evelyn was a little shy about not only being a bystander, but also touching herself while observing. She felt like one of those perverts who secretly watched people through windows while jerking off. The difference here was that they wanted her there, wanted her to watch and they wanted her to come with them.

She found she wanted that too.

"It's just like watching porn," she assured herself. "You rub one out all the time while watching others fuck. You just happen to have a front-row seat this time," she muttered.

She threw a sheet over herself. It helped her feel less exposed. That thin layer of privacy allowed her to move her hand down along her body, resting it on top of her panties. She played with the outline of her lips while she watched the scene escalate in front of her.

When she looked up, her shadow was on her knees, deep-throating his cock, while cupping his ass. Evelyn slid down her panties, dipped her finger in her wet cunt, then rubbed her clit. She came at the same time he did, as if he were waiting for her.

When he was finished spilling down her throat, (She assumed. The jury was still out on whether he could actually ejaculate) he walked them over to the bed. He surprised Evelyn by lying beside her. He turned his head towards her, and she swore he winked at her (or would have if he had eyes) before he guided her shadow to straddle his head, and lowered her pussy onto his wanting mouth.

Evelyn grabbed the vibrator. It was her favourite. It had various degrees of sucking, mimicking cunnilingus. It was almost as good as the real thing.

Almost.

It lasted longer though. It didn't get lockjaw, and she could play with it for hours. Truth be told, sometimes she preferred this toy to the real thing.

She let the vibrator work its magic on her cunt while she watched him eat out her shadow's. His hands dug into her hips helping her move to ride his mouth.

This time Evelyn came with her shadow.

Her orgasm was so intense, that her body flushed with intense heat. Modesty forgotten, she threw the sheet off to find some relief as she came down from the euphoric high.

Her shadow didn't have time to catch her breath. (Do shadows breathe?) He lifted her by the hips, taking her off his mouth and planted her on his long, girthy, hard, veiny (Evelyn imagined) throbbing cock. She started circling her hips and rocking back and forth, instantly encouraging Evelyn to try for orgasm number three.

Evelyn was captivated by her shadow's bouncing tits as she rode the sexually deviant prowler. Her arousal peaked, watching her breast move and jiggle as she rode his shaft.

Is this weird? she thought, as she started reaching toward another peak. *They're practically mine...from this perspective though, I must admit, my tits look fucking amazing. I would motorboat them.*

Evelyn was about to come again when she looked over and found his head turned towards her. He was on the precipice, watching Evelyn watch her own shadow's body on display. He reached towards her, moving slowly like he was giving her time to reject his touch.

Surprising herself, she welcomed it and made no move to shy away.

He placed his hand on her hip bone, giving soft squeezes as they all rose and climaxed together.

When the shadows finished, he gave Evelyn's hip one last squeeze, then helped her shadow off his lap, and walked her over to the wall. They shared the night's final kiss, and then he helped her step back into the wall where she resumed her non-sentient existence.

Evelyn watched this, sprawled out half-naked lying in a huge wet spot of her own making. She was so thoroughly satisfied, that she didn't care what he was seeing as he stood beside the bed studying her. But she felt safe with him. He wasn't judging. If anything, if he had a face, she knew he would be giving her an arrogant smoulder.

He brought his hand to his mouth, blew her a kiss, (at least made the gesture), gave her a slight bow, and then dissolved into the surrounding shadows.

CHAPTER SIX

Otherworldly Gazette

Article

Shadow People

Shadow people have been plaguing our peripherals for decades. Experiences vary between witnesses. Some merely explained they had seen a flash of movement at the corner of their eye, but when they turned their head, nothing was there. Others claimed to have seen something from a faint shadow walking by, to a more solid humanoid presence. Evidence has been reportedly caught on tape of this phenomenon, but in these modern times of special effects and film manipulation, so easily done now with just a cell phone, it is hard to sift through what is fake or genuine.

The consensus as to what this phenomenon could be is that there is no consensus.

The scientific community believes that our brains manifest this experience partly due to mental health disorders. When the left temporoparietal junction is stimulated, it can create illusions or experiences that aren't real. Shadow people encounters are common among people who suffer from psychotic disorders such as schizophrenia and paranoia.

But not everyone with a psychotic disorder is having these experiences.

The paranormal experts and community don't believe there is a simple scientific answer for these occurrences. While they can all agree that there is more than science at play, experts are divided as to what these shadow people actually could be.

Experts originally cried ghosts. It was the easiest explanation. Apparitions have been documented for as long as the written word has been recorded. Some argued that while they may look like ghosts, their actions differ. Many have reported that these shadows have followed them throughout their lives, attaching to a person, not a place.

A popular theory is demons. They are used to explain the more opaque humanoid sightings. Experts claim that demons latch onto one's soul, and believe they eventually will cause harm to the possessed, as well as others around them. Cleansing rituals and exorcisms are routinely performed by religious leaders to rid the demons and send them back to hell where they believe they are from.

Aliens and other dimensional beings are another theory gaining ground. Some will argue that they are the same thing. It is believed in the scientific and paranormal communities that there are bridges between dimensions, and these beings are able to find the rifts and navigate through them.

Finally, some experts and witnesses believe shadow people cannot be lumped into the above categories and that they are a separate phenomenon.

. . .

Sexual Shadow Experiences

Aliens abduct, ghosts haunt, demons possess, and shadow people have been known to be sexually aggressive.

Witnesses have come forward with claims that they have had sexual encounters with shadow people. Some experiences were pleasant, while others claimed to have been raped. These humanoid beings were able to change their forms at will, allowing them to pass through objects one minute, and become as solid as humans the next.

Sexual frustration, unplanned celibacy, deep depression, persistent self-consciousness, extreme self-loathing and self-doubt, and loneliness. These conditions have all been attributed to summoning a sexual shadow person.

Some victims, who don't consider themselves victims at all, felt empathy from these beings, and had what they called a romantic experience with them. They were left feeling wanted, loved and satisfied.

. . .

The majority of victims claimed to have been assaulted. They were often woken in the middle of the night, feeling someone on top of them. They were impossible to fight off, and the victims were eventually violated by penetration. When the assailants were finished, they vanished before their victims' eyes.

Night terrors are a common theory to try to explain these experiences, except it doesn't explain why victims wake up with sore genitals and anus.

One thing experts in the scientific, paranormal, and religious fields can agree on, is that more research needs to be done.

If you have had an experience with a shadow person, please reach out. You can find our contact form on our resources page.

CHAPTER SEVEN

"I don't know if I should feel relieved or crazy," Evelyn muttered to herself, after reading a few articles she found about the shadow people phenomenon.

She spent the morning ignoring emails and searching the strange corners of the internet. Last night convinced her that her handsome, hollowed, humanoid lover was real, and not a lucid dream. She had woken that morning half-naked, vibrator beside her, feeling thoroughly satisfied.

A part of her wanted, no, needed to understand what he was, what was happening, and why. Yet, another part of her didn't want to question it any further and just go with it. She couldn't explain how, but after last night she knew he would never hurt her.

"It's the perfect situation, really," she said aloud as she closed all her browser tabs and wiped her search history. "I don't have to go on terrible dates, spend money, dress up nice, or even talk. He comes to me, we fuck, and he leaves. Well, fucks my shadow..."

She looked beside her, where her shadow was hunched over

its own shadowy workstation. Resentment and bitterness heavy in her glare.

Envy. She was envious of her shadow.

She shook her head and cleared her mind.

"This is ridiculous! This entire thing is ridiculous," she said, with a nervous chuckle.

Ridiculous, but she secretly hoped that the tantalizing transparent trespasser would continue his escalation, and didn't leave her behind to play voyeur for another night.

I need to get my hands and mouth wrapped around that cock.

Her clit started throbbing from the memory of his dick rubbing against her shadow's stomach as he kissed up and down her body.

I'll fucking rub it over my entire face, she thought, when there was a knock at her office door.

"Knock knock," Brock said as he entered before Evelyn had the chance to invite him in. "Mmm, look at you, blushing already."

Evelyn's arousal had caused her skin to flush.

Perfect fucking timing as always, Brock.

"Right...it's just hot in my office today. I'm regretting this sweater."

"I'm regretting it too," he said, as his eyes trailed down her body. "Whatever happened to that purple blouse you wore that one time? I remember it being a rather chilly day," he said, eyebrows wagging.

Evelyn knew exactly what blouse he was talking about. It was a beautiful lightweight cotton top that she bought for the extreme summer temperatures. She was one hundred percent positive that Brock turned up the air conditioner that morning when he saw her enter the office wearing it and failed to look her in the eye for the remainder of the day. That blouse had been shoved to the back of her closet, reserved for non-work-related outings.

"Was there something you needed, Brock?" Evelyn asked, trying to bring the conversation back to an appropriate subject.

"Well, it's almost noon, and I haven't seen my favourite IT manager, so I wanted to say good morning."

Because I was avoiding you, she thought.

"That's very kind of you, but if you will excuse me, I have a lot of work tickets to get through."

Brock ignored her, and sat down in one of the two chairs that faced her desk, sitting opposite of her.

"Did I see you walk out yesterday with Eric Stirling?"

"We walked out together, yes," Evelyn answered.

"Why?" Brock scoffed.

"What do you mean why? He was leaving, I was leaving. It would have been rude to ignore him."

"Why did he insist on keeping you in the meeting yesterday? Have you met him before?"

"No, we met yesterday when he took a wrong turn trying to find the conference room, and as he explained to you, he wanted all management present, to make a better-informed decision on whether he wanted to work with our company or not."

"I don't like it," Brock admitted.

"What is it you don't like, exactly?"

"Did he ask you out?" Brock asked, irritation and warning heavy in his voice.

"No, but would it be any of your business if he had?" Evelyn asked, defiance evident in her tone.

"As a matter of fact, it would. I can't have you fucking every important potential client who walks through our office door. What if something goes wrong? What if your pussy isn't good enough to hold his interest, you have a bad breakup, and he decides he can't bear to see your face anymore and terminates our working relationship. He is so wealthy that the monetary penalty for breaking our contract is like fucking milk money to him. So yeah, I'm going to make it my business if you want to act like a whore."

"Jesus, Brock, you can't speak to me that way!"

"Go cry to your boss, oh wait, that's me," he laughed. "Did. He. Ask. You. Out?" Brock asked again, enunciating every word.

"No, he didn't," Evelyn answered, just above a whisper. She was trying to keep it together. She refused to show Brock that his inappropriate and possessive behaviour was getting to her.

"Of course he didn't," he sighed. "Why would a man with that much wealth and success be interested in a woman who makes sure our wifi bill is paid?"

With a cruel smile, he stood up, walked over to Evelyn's side, and sat on her desk.

"Look babe, I don't mean to be cruel. I'm just giving you a reality check. If you were to cost our company a client like him, I would have to sack you. Then I would make sure you couldn't get a job fetching coffee in your cute little blouses and skirts in this city or the next. Stay in your lane, stay cute, and just keep my copiers and phones working." He had reached out and lightly placed his hand under her chin, rubbing his thumb back in forth. He spoke like he was comforting a child. His tone mocking.

"And one day you will realize that you can't do better than me. You won't do better than me. I won't allow it. If you want to keep this job, you will either become a lonely spinster, or come crawling to my office, on all fours where you belong, begging to finally suck my cock, and let me own you. The choice is yours," he said, just above a whisper, not wanting his voice to carry, and giving her chin a slight squeeze.

Evelyn jerked her head out of his grasp. She had a retort

ready on the tip of her tongue, but Brock got up and left, giving her a knowing wink before he closed the door behind him.

Evelyn's lower lip started to quiver. She hated that she cried when she was frustrated or angry. It made her feel weak and out of control. Once the first tear spilled, she couldn't keep it in any longer. She ran to lock her door, worried that someone would see her in this state. After a few minutes, when she could string a sentence together without sobbing, she called her boss, her other boss, Brock's brother Charles, and let him know that she wasn't feeling well and would be out of the office the rest of the day.

Evelyn was responsible for four employees. She never took time off or abused her position and often took care of jobs that her lower employees should be doing. Charles had no problem letting her go and reminded her that she worked too hard.

Evelyn thanked Charles, biting her tongue.

Charles was a great boss. Or would have been if he didn't turn a blind eye to his little brother's unprofessional, indecent behaviour. Brock had never gotten in trouble. He knows how to clean up his messes, and is very good with blackmail, so Charles lets him have free reign. Plus Brock is charismatic and can talk anyone into anything, which is great for business, so Charles will take the good and ignore the bad.

Which is why no one will bring Brock's behaviour to his attention. But he knows, at least to some extent, and that makes him complicit.

Evelyn cleaned up her face enough so she could leave her office and the building without having someone ask her what was wrong. When she exited the front doors she nearly ran to her car. She was hoping to wait until she got to her apartment to fall apart, but her car would have to do.

CHAPTER EIGHT

Wine.

All the wine.

Evelyn spent the rest of the day crying, drinking, and brainstorming.

She got the ugly crying out of the way first. She curled up in a ball on her couch and let the tears flow, the snot run, and the spit fly. It was cathartic and cleared her mind.

With a few glasses of wine and her laptop, she spent hours trying to figure out how to outsmart Brock.

Option A. She could try to get him fired for sexual harassment, but that didn't seem likely at this point. He was too well protected. He was too attractive. There were women impatiently biding their time, waiting their turn for that asshole to turn his attention to them. If she tried to complain to HR, they would tell her she was lucky, and shouldn't complain to have someone like Brock giving her attention. (They have all had their turn with him.) Charles won't help. He was too protective of his brother and their company. So option A was out of the question.

Option B. She needed to leave. But how?

Brock made it clear that he would make her life a living hell if she were to date anyone else. She would be out of a job, and he had the connections and means to damage Evelyn's reputation to the point beyond repair. When he said she wouldn't even be able to serve coffee, he meant it.

Brock was becoming too much, and it was starting to scare her. His obscene behaviour was escalating to the point of obsession. He would never let her have a relationship again, and the alternative made her gag. He didn't want a relationship. He wanted to possess her. Own her. Be able to fuck her whenever he wanted. He would be able to fool around with others, but she would have to be available only to him, whenever he pleased.

"If he weren't such a dick, and willing and able to ruin my life, that would kind of almost be fun, except for the whole 'I couldn't screw other people part,'" she said aloud, pouring another glass of wine.

"Stupid hot bosses. Bosses shouldn't be allowed to be so stupid hot," she slurred.

After she cursed Brock's looks and her confused sexual attraction to him for another half hour, she came up with a plan.

Staying at this job was not an option. Staying single out of fear of losing her job and having her professional reputation trashed just couldn't happen. Giving into Brock, despite his looks and carnal expertise, was absolutely never going to happen. She was sure he wouldn't even allow her to quit with advanced notice and on good terms. She would have to play the long game.

She estimated that her plan would take at least a year. She would have to move to another city, so she would need time to save some money. This time would be spent researching Brock and Charles' reach. This shouldn't be hard to do. She had access to all their emails, contracts, etc. If there was a digital footprint, she could access it. She could have a new job in a new city lined up before they had time to realize she was leaving. The only difficult part of this plan would be the waiting. A year of avoiding Brock's advances and playing nice to keep her job would be a test of her strength and character, but she was up for the challenge.

Evelyn stumbled to the shower, feeling a bit better now that she could see some kind of end in sight.

A year isn't that long, she thought, trying to convince herself she could do this.

What choice did she have?

The shower sobered her up a little, and, even though she felt better about her predicament, she still felt down and a bit defeated when she finally climbed into bed.

"Eric...," she sighed, as she settled in. "What do I do about you?"

Doubt flooded her thoughts. Eric acted like he was interested. All the signs were there. But what if Brock was right? Why would a multi-millionaire be interested in a woman who works IT? Sure, she was attractive. Some have called her the total package, but as she web-searched him, she saw pictures of Eric at galas with women who must be models hanging off his arm. She couldn't find two pictures of him with the same woman. Was he just another serial dater?

"Why do I attract these kinds of men?" she groaned, throwing her phone on the charger and rolling over. She was mentally exhausted and was done with thinking for the night.

When Evelyn felt the bed shift a few hours later, she woke up to a feeling of anticipation and a little bit of relief. After the day she had, she could use a few intense orgasms. She was already lying on her back, so she turned her head slowly to greet her lucid lover.

She was surprised to see her shadow already awake and moving independently. He was able to access her without waking Evelyn up. They were both sitting beside her, her shadow closer to her feet, and the shadowy man near her head.

"I hope I didn't miss anything," Evelyn said.

To her surprise, they both shook their heads no in response.

"Great, let me just grab my—"

She was reaching towards her nightstand to grab her favourite vibrator when she felt a hand squeeze her leg, bringing her attention back to them.

"You don't want me to grab it?"

They both shook their heads no.

"Do you want me to just watch again?" she asked, a little disheartened by the thought of not taking part. She sat up, waiting for the answer.

They both shook their heads no, again.

"I don't understand," Evelyn admitted. A sob escaped, which surprised her. She was confused but she didn't think she would cry over something like this.

The shadow man lifted his arm and slowly brought his hand to her face. He started stroking her cheeks lightly with his thumb. After a moment of enjoying his caress, she realized he was wiping away tears. He pulled his hand away, and placed his hand in front of her, as if to show her the tears, and asked what was wrong.

"I didn't realize I was crying," Evelyn said, wiping her eyes.

Evelyn felt her leg being tapped and saw that her shadow was trying to get her attention. She clasped her hands together, bringing them to the side of her head, mimicking sleep, then dragged her finger down its face, to show tears.

"Was I crying in my sleep?" Evelyn asked.

They both nodded yes, her shadow placing their hand over their heart, showing their sympathy for her.

"It was a rough day," Evelyn said to them. "I just have a lot going on. Life will be a little tough for a while. It's okay if you don't want me to play tonight. I get it."

They shook their heads no, then looked at each other, having a silent conversation. When they returned their attention to Evelyn, they made the same gesture; they pointed to Evelyn, and then to each other.

Evelyn tried to speak, wanting further clarification as to what they were trying to communicate to her, but the shadow man placed his finger to her mouth to prevent her from speaking further. He then caressed her cheek once more.

His touch was unique. It was warm, yet cool, and left a tingling sensation that lingered for a brief moment. It reminded her of that lube she bought that one time that promised the same sensation, except it just left her pussy burning for hours.

He placed his hand on her shoulder, pushing gently, guiding her to lie down.

What the hell, she thought. She was done questioning and was eager to find out what they had in mind for her that night.

He leaned over her, his hand tenderly caressing her face again, but this time, he didn't stop at her chin. His fingers played along her jaw, caressed her ear and trailed down her neck until his palm lay flat against her chest.

Then he grabbed her throat.

He didn't squeeze but held her firm. He used his index finger to tilt her head back, and then with the utmost control, he lowered his mouth to hers, stopping with only a breath's space left between them.

Evelyn tried to close the space, desperate for her lips to touch. Touch what? She wasn't exactly sure, but she needed to find out. He tightened his grip, just enough to deny her movement.

She felt a hot shadowing breath as he teased her, brushing his now solid mouth along her lips, ear and neck.

Fuck, he has the perfect mouth, she thought as he drove her wild with anticipation.

He had full pouty lips that were begging to be kissed, licked, sucked, and nibbled and Evelyn was more than willing to do her part. She was so focused on this new development that she forgot about her shadow, until she felt hands trailing up her thighs, followed by kisses.

A moan escaped her lips. Then a sob.

This is all for me, she realized. Before another sob could break free, he brought his lips down onto hers, swallowing her sorrow.

His kiss was soft, slow and tender but quickly escalated. She opened her mouth, inviting him in deeper and was pleasantly surprised to find a tongue pushing back onto hers. He released her neck and found the hem of her tank top. He pushed it up until her breasts were exposed, nipples hard, each begging for attention.

As her top went up, her panties went down. Her shadow removed her underwear, soaked with arousal, and restarted her kissing ascent up her thighs.

My shadow is about to eat my pussy! she thought. She found herself more excited by this prospect than not. She had fingered herself more times than she could count. If she were flexible, she would probably lick her own cunt if she could.

As he brought his mouth down onto her nipple, her shadow brought hers down onto Evelyn's clit.

The sensation was almost too much. Her shadow expertly used her mouth, the hot/cold sensation edging her quickly towards an orgasm, while her tits were being thoroughly squeezed by his large strong hands while being nibbled, licked and sucked. At that moment, she felt taken care of, cherished, safe. She didn't want this to end, afraid if she came, she would unravel emotionally again.

Let go.

It wasn't said out loud. A man's husky voice penetrated her mind. It was so faint, she wasn't sure if she imagined it herself, but she knew she didn't. He wanted her to give in, hand herself fully over to them.

She let go.

Together, the sensual silhouettes guided her through her intense climax. Her shadow was relentless in her assault on her clit, getting the most out of her orgasm, while large firm hands kept her pinned down until they were sure she was finished riding the wave of pleasure.

A single tear rolled down Evelyn's face. She needed that. Not just the orgasm, but that entire release. She couldn't remember the last time she had completely surrendered herself like that. Had someone, or in this case, some *things*, who cared more about her pleasure, her needs, above their own. She didn't care how the rest of the night progressed, there was no coming down from her current euphoric state.

But they were just getting started.

Her penumbra playmates kept to the evening's theme of keeping Evelyn the primary focus. Sometimes they made her lay there, to just enjoy the pleasure they were enthusiastic to give, trading places, so he got a chance to eat her out while her shadow got to play with the rest of her. In other instances, they followed Evelyn's lead. She was eager to get her hands on his massive shady shaft. She rubbed it all over her face, before taking the entire length down her throat while she sat on his face, having her pussy eaten from behind.

Evelyn was worried that her desires, and theirs, would get

lost in their nonverbal communication, but they were so attuned to one another. They moved as one, synchronized, anticipating each other's wants and needs. When she wanted to have her face buried in her shadow's cunt while being slammed from behind, it was a natural progression. It was as if they could read her mind, predicting everything she wanted.

They also knew when Evelyn needed rest.

She would have carried on all night and endured the consequences tomorrow. Being exhausted, suffering through a workday barely coherent with deep purple bags under her eyes would be worth it. She didn't want the night to end. Although this night was giving her what she wanted, it was also about providing her with what she needed. She needed this release, she needed to feel wanted, and now she needed sleep so she could face this new challenge with Brock and come out ahead.

Evelyn watched as her shadow was escorted back into the wall by the magnanimous mystery man. When it was settled back to its inanimate state, he walked through the bed, to the other side where Evelyn sat, back leaning against her headboard.

"Thank you," Evelyn whispered. "I don't know who or what you are, or where you come from, but I don't think it matters to me anymore. Whether you were sent, or came on your own, I am just so grateful that you are here."

He sat on the bed beside her and cupped the side of her face with one hand in response.

"I'm sorry I was so frightened before. Will you come back?"

He removed his hand and picked up her cell phone. He held it up, wanting her to unlock it. Once obliged, he showed her the screen she already had up. An image search of Eric Stirling. He pointed to a professional picture of Eric.

"What about him? Brock was right, there is no way

someone like Eric would be interested in me. Besides, even if he was, I'm stuck. Brock has me completely trapped."

The shadow shook his head in disagreement and pointed to the picture once more before putting it back on her nightstand. He held the side of her face once more before leaning in, giving her a tender kiss on the lips, and one more on her forehead before he was gone, fading away into the night.

CHAPTER NINE

"It's open."

Evelyn spent the first few hours of the day prioritizing and answering emails and work tickets. She woke up that morning with a clear mind and a new determination. For the next year, she would work hard, keep her head down, and avoid Brock as much as she could, or as much as he allowed it. She wanted to remain under the radar, while she secretly put her plan into action. She would not give her bosses a reason to question her work or her loyalty to the company. She would also have to be careful when she investigated how connected the brothers were. She wasn't naive and suspected they had hired outside, private professionals to safeguard their private files, emails and texts.

No one knew about her hacking abilities.

The was a soft knock before the door opened halfway, and Eric poked his head through.

"Is this a bad time?" he asked with a smirk.

"Not at all. Are you lost again?" she chuckled.

"No, this time I'm exactly where I need to be," he answered, giving her a shy smile. He held up a cardboard tray, holding two coffees. "Regular coffee, two creams, one sugar, right?"

"Yes," Evelyn said, disbelief in her voice.

"Why do you seem so surprised?" he asked. "You said yes to coffee, right?"

Eric's confident posture deflated. He looked nervously at Eveyln, and then down at the tray, worried he was screwing this up.

"I'm just a bit surprised you remembered, that's all." She looked down shyly at her hands, playing with her fingers, as Brock's words echoed in her mind before she continued. "You are a very important, busy man. I wasn't going to hold you to it if you forgot."

"Forget?" Eric started laughing in relief. "There was no way I was going to forget. It's all I've been thinking about, actually," he said, looking intently into her eyes.

They drank the coffee in Evelyn's office. He had asked what her preference was; going for a walk or staying put. She chose the latter, to avoid being seen by Brock, or anyone who would gossip.

Eric was very attentive, wanting to know about Evelyn, from where she grew up, to her favourite music and food. He was very interested in learning about her role and responsibilities at Collins Industries, and only interrupted her to ask clarifying questions, showing he was not only actively listening, but was eager to learn more.

"Oh my goodness, I have been doing all the talking," Evelyn said, slightly abashed, cheeks reddening, as she realized the time. They had been talking for forty-five minutes. "I promise I'm not this self-centred!"

"Please, I wish I had time to hear more," he admitted.

"I have so many questions for you," Evelyn said, as she noticed Eric check his watch.

"The contract negotiations start in a few minutes, but maybe we can continue this later? Replace the coffee with wine? Your office, with a nice restaurant?"

"I would love that, but..." she started and trailed off. She couldn't say yes. It didn't matter how much she wanted to.

"Walk me to the conference room again?" he asked, lips pulled into a grin, mischief in his eyes.

He's up to something, Evelyn thought.

She had a feeling he knew she wasn't invited to this negotiation, as she was not invited to the sales pitch. Evelyn shook her head and laughed.

"Yes, of course," she replied, unable to keep the amusement off her face.

Showing up with Eric, uninvited again, would not help her efforts to stay quiet and unnoticed, but she could argue that she couldn't deny the request of a potential client who wanted to be escorted around the office.

Plus she couldn't deny wanting to see Brock, Charles, and all the other executives squirm and bend over backwards at Eric's demands again. Even if she were going to pay for it later when Eric left.

Evelyn stopped outside of the conference room. Everyone was already inside, waiting for Eric.

"Good luck in there," she said, before lowering her voice to a whisper. "They are willing to give you everything you want, so keep playing hardball," she said with a wink.

She turned to walk away, but Eric stopped her by gently grabbing onto her arm above her elbow. She turned around, looked down at his hand that held her arm, then back at him expectantly. They shared an intimate gaze for a few moments, both affected by this sudden contact. Eric reluctantly removed his hand and cleared his throat.

"Aren't you coming in with me?"

"Mr. Stirling, you know—" she started.

"Eric," he reminded her.

"Eric," she corrected. "You know I wasn't—"

"Mr. Stirling! Perfect timing as always," Brock said, interrupting their exchange. "Do you need something, Ms. Jones?"

"I was just walking Mr. Stirling to the conference room," she explained, keeping a polite and professional tone.

"Actually, I was just telling Evelyn that I wanted her to sit in on the negotiations," Eric said.

Ugh, don't use my first name around him.

"I assure you that *Evelyn*, won't be needed today," Brock argued back, wearing his best fake negotiating smile.

"I insist," Eric asserted. He stared at Brock with a slight smile, but all humour and friendliness were gone. Negotiations had already begun, and they started with Evelyn.

"After you," Brock conceded, stepping aside to allow Eric into the boardroom first. Evelyn went to follow, but Brock blocked her entry.

"You and I are going to have a little talk later," he whispered in her ear, before letting her by, and not giving her much room to do so.

Evelyn kept her head down and continued walking. Eric insisted she sit beside him once more, and she kept her eyes down, ready to take notes on her phone, trying to ignore the heat of Brock's stare.

Negotiations were tough and slated to last hours. Eric was well prepared. He spoke with knowledge, confidence, assurance, and the right touch of arrogance. Everything he said was careful and calculated, and his voice demanded attention.

Evelyn found it irresistibly sexy.

Panties wet.

Eric's deep velvety voice was like a beacon. Every time he

spoke up, commanding the room, Evelyn unconsciously inched closer towards him. She remained unaware of her proximity to him until she caught Brock's angry glare. He was shooting daggers at her, his eyes bounced between hers, and where her arm was resting casually against Eric's.

Evelyn pretended she needed to adjust her blazer's sleeve, and then placed her arm beside, but not touching, Eric's. Eric noticed the absence of her touch. He looked at Evelyn whose eyes were cast down, unfocused, and then looked across the table in time to see Brock's penetrating glare before he shifted his focus back on the paperwork.

A few hours into the meeting Eric called for a break. He had a few phone calls he needed to make, and everyone agreed to meet back in an hour.

Charles showed Eric to an empty office he could use, while everyone was discussing lunch orders, which allowed Evelyn to sneak out unnoticed. She went back to her office to gather her laptop, a notepad, and pens to bring back to the meeting. She had an hour to waste, so she checked her e-mail to make sure nothing was pressing.

There was.

She received an alert that one of the servers was malfunctioning. All her employees were busy dealing with a major malware issue. Someone thought it would be a good idea to not only watch porn at work, but to send a few clips to their friends. "Plumber Cleans Out Milf's Pipes" sent a nasty virus that was now plaguing their entire system.

The server would be an easy fix, so she would just handle it herself. The server room was on the way to the boardroom, so she packed up her laptop bag so she wouldn't have to double back to her office. She could have the problem fixed, and get back to the boardroom with plenty of time to spare.

The server room was small, around the size of a large walk-in closet. She quickly found what needed to be fixed and went to work getting it back online.

"I usually prefer you in a skirt, but I have to admit, these slacks are working for me."

Evelyn, who had her back to the door, whipped around to find Brock's broad figure filling the doorway.

"You're not in your office," Brock stated. "Are you avoiding me?"

It took all of Evelyn's willpower not to roll her eyes. She knew she was already on shaky ground. She needed to be careful, not to add any fuel to the fire.

"There is an issue with one of the servers, so I'm getting it back online before negotiations resume," she answered, desperately trying to keep the "what does it look like I'm doing" inflection out of her voice.

"About that...did you already forget about our little chat? Was I not clear yesterday?" he sneered.

"Crystal."

"Then what the fuck are you doing practically sitting on Eric Stirling's lap in a meeting you have no business attending?"

"He asked that I accompany him," she said, shrugging, trying to play it cool, like it was no big deal. She had a slight tremor in her voice and hoped Brock didn't pick up on it. "I'm just doing what is asked, being a team player so negotiations go smoothly. This contract will be huge for the company."

"You fucked him." Not a question, but an accusation.

"What? No!"

Brock moved into the small room, not slowing his advancement until he had Evelyn pinned against a server tower. He placed one hand beside her head, blocking her way of escape.

"Did he ask you out?" Brock asked, leaning in close.

"I won't...I won't go out with him," Evelyn responded. She was unable to keep her voice from shaking now and hated herself for it. She didn't want Brock to see how he was affecting her. She turned her head away, avoiding Brock's intense stare.

"That's not what I asked, babe," he reminded her, dragging his nose up her exposed neck.

Evelyn shuddered from the intimate touch. A few days ago she would have been tempted to give in and let him have her, but now she felt nothing but repulsion. She had her hands balled at her sides, and kept utterly still, hoping he would get to his point and quickly move along.

Brock took his free hand and grabbed her chin, turning her head, and forcing her to look up at him.

"Enjoy his attention while it lasts. You are nothing to him but a pretty face and a tight ass for him to play with while he spends time in this office. Once he is finished solidifying this deal, do you really think you will see him again?"

Evelyn didn't answer, but the sheen in her eyes and the slight quiver in her bottom lip betrayed her.

"You poor pathetic little whore. You *did* think he liked you, didn't you?" he snickered. "I honestly don't know whether to laugh or just feel sorry for you."

He tightened his grip on her chin. It was painful and she knew it would cause bruising, but she would not give him the satisfaction of showing any discomfort. Nor would she respond to what he said. She stared back defiantly.

"Fuck Evelyn, just stop fighting this and let me have you. You are being such a stubborn cunt about all this," he said as he roughly released her chin, causing her head to snap back and lightly hit the tower behind her. "The position you find yourself in is all on you, you know that, right?"

"This isn't the conference room."

Brock pushed off the wall and spun around to meet Eric,

while Evelyn moved to face the server, continuing, or trying to continue her work. She didn't want Eric to see how upset she was and needed a moment to compose herself.

"Mr. Stirling, I hope you are more savvy at business than you are with your sense of direction," Brock said, instantly turning on the charm with his best fake laughter.

"I promise, you won't be disappointed," Eric replied, his voice was friendly but there was no mistaking the implied warning.

"Shall I walk you back then?" Brock asked, already moving towards the door with his arm outstretched, ready to usher Eric out.

"Actually, I'd like to learn more about what Evelyn is doing right now," he said to Brock. Then he turned to Evelyn. "I can trust you to get me back on time, right?"

"Whatever you need, Mr. Stirling," she said over her shoulder. She was worried her face still showed too much emotion, so she couldn't face both men just yet.

"Right, sure, of course. I'll see you in there, then." Brock said, barely able to keep the annoyance out of his tone.

Eric waited a few moments after Brock left before he turned to Evelyn.

"Are you okay?"

"Fine, this is just a quick job. A simple reboot," Evelyn replied as she worked.

"Evelyn...," he said, voice lowered and gentle. She stilled for a brief moment but didn't turn around. She continued working. "Evelyn, I overheard practically everything, please, look at me," he pleaded.

Evelyn slowly turned around. Her cheeks were flushed with embarrassment. She looked at him quickly, then averted her gaze to the floor, too ashamed to keep eye contact with him.

"When you said a Brock was giving you trouble, you meant *that* Brock? Your boss?"

"It's fine, I'm handling it," she assured him.

"Handling what? What exactly does he have over you?"

Evelyn shook her head. "Please, just let it go," she whispered.

"Have you reported his behaviour?"

"It's a complicated situation, I don't want to talk about it. I told you, I'm handling it."

"Why not just leave?" he asked.

Evelyn looked up at him, willing her eyes to stay dry as they pleaded with him to let it go.

"You can't, can you?"

"Without going into details, no, he has made it practically impossible," she admitted.

He used a finger to gently raise her chin, noticing the red marks on her face where Brock had grabbed her. She watched his features change from compassion to rage.

"You're quitting, right now. You are undervalued here anyway. Let me take care of you."

Evelyn turned her head to remove Eric's hand. "No."

"No? Do you want to stay here and continue getting sexually assaulted?"

"Of course, I don't want to stay," Evelyn whisper-shouted, worried their argument would carry out to the hall. "But I also don't need to be saved by some rich and powerful hot guy, who has a different model on his arm at every event, and who was just going to forget about me after his business concluded."

"Jesus fuck, Evelyn! Brock has you so brainwashed," Eric whisper-shouted back. "I haven't dated anyone in years. And in all the pictures you see when you search my name were just random people at events I attended. People asked to take a photo with me, so I obliged."

Relief washed over Evelyn.

So he is single and doesn't date models. Or at least hasn't recently. Shit...focus...

"And I am so torn because at first, I was interested in dating you. I mean, I still am, but I also see your potential being wasted here, so now I'm also interested in you professionally, and I do my very best not to cross lines."

"I...I don't know what to say. I'm so sorry that I allowed Brock to get inside my head. That I didn't believe my gut, and I let him make me believe that your intentions were so untoward."

"I just need you to tell me when you can leave. You said you have a plan?"

"The soonest would be a year, but that depends if I can save up enough to move."

"Move? How much influence does he have in this city?" he asked, voice seething.

"Too much."

Eric started to pace the small room in quiet contemplation. He abruptly stopped and turned to Evelyn, having come to some decision.

"Can you do me a favour and tell everyone in the boardroom that I will be a few minutes late?" he asked.

"Yes, of course," she nodded. "Do you want me to relay a reason, or just say you will be late?"

"Well, you can't tell them I need a few minutes to calm down," he laughed. "But I'm going to make a few more phone calls, so if you can tell them that, I would appreciate it."

"Consider it done," she said, as she grabbed her bag and started towards the conference room.

"Evelyn." Eric stopped her before she left. "When I get back to the boardroom, I better see you sitting down at the table. If they give you a hard time about being there, make it clear that I will walk out of here. This company needs me more than I need them." Eric stated, a mischievous grin plastered on his face.

"Understood," she replied.

As she walked away, the corners of her mouth lifted. She was eager to see how this would all play out.

CHAPTER TEN

E velyn arrived at the boardroom, relayed Eric's message that he would be a few minutes late, and apologized on his behalf.

"Thanks, Evelyn, you may go," Brock said, waving his hand in dismissal.

Did he just shoo me away? Fucking prick.

"Mr. Stirling is insisting I stay," she informed him, trying to keep the wry smile off her face. She may have been untouchable when Eric was around, but Brock would take the first opportunity to haul her aside and wipe that, and any future smiles off her face.

"Ms. Jones, I'm not having this argument with you," Brock said.

Evelyn turned to Charles, who was silently watching their exchange.

"He wanted me to make it clear, that if he returns and I'm not here, he will walk out the door and the deal will be off."

"What kind of a power play is he pulling? Why are you worth so much to him?" Brock snapped, losing his cool.

"Careful brother," Charles warned under his breath. "Mr.

Stirling's associates are sitting right there, and lawyers tend to have superb hearing in these kinds of environments."

Brock took his seat in protest, unable to refute what his brother just said.

"Take a seat, Evelyn. Hopefully, we will be starting soon," Charles said.

Evelyn sat down and powered up her laptop as she waited for negotiations to resume. When she looked up, she found Brock staring at her, a wicked smile stretched across his face. It was unnerving. Her mind started to race, envisioning everything he could do to retaliate against her insubordination.

Would he go as far as to rape her?

There have been many rumours about him, and most have been proven true, (no one believed that he satisfied four women at the same time, and everyone is sure he started that one), but not once have there been any whispers of anything non-consensual. At the same time, being in his position, he could make assault and rape allegations go away before the rumours had a chance to start. With the way he was looking at her at that moment, she didn't think he had cornering and begging her to let him perform oral sex in mind.

The room started to tilt, and she found she couldn't breathe.

Evelyn contemplated excusing herself, but she knew she was currently in the safest place she could be. She would not underestimate Brock. He would follow her, and for the first time, she was afraid.

Eric walked in.

He wore his professional mask; confidence, determination, and arrogance lined his features, but Evelyn noticed his eyes twinge with relief for the briefest of moments when he saw her sitting at the long conference table.

"Ladies and Gentleman, I apologize for the delay," he said, addressing the full room, as he sat down beside Evelyn.

Although he didn't address her directly, when he sat down her anxiety eased by his proximity and she was able to take her first proper breath since she entered the room.

"I believe we left off at article four, section three," Charles began, jumping right back into the meeting.

"Mr. Collins," Eric interrupted, and the sound of paper shuffling halted. When he had everyone's attention, he continued. "I'm going to save us all a very boring afternoon. My terms are simple. You give me everything I want outlined in the contract my lawyers had originally drafted, because it's fair, and you know that it is. Do that and release Ms. Jones into my employment, and we will have a deal." Eric stood up, motioning his entourage to do the same.

Evelyn gasped.

"Absolutely not!" Brock barked, slamming his hand onto the desk. Everyone looked up at him, surprised by his outburst. Realizing his mistake, he took a deep breath before he continued. "Ms. Jones is vital to our operation here at Collins Industries. We can't let her go."

"Yet you fought against her attendance at these *vital* meetings," Eric replied, arching his eyebrow, waiting for a rebuttal.

"Has she agreed to this?" Charles chimed in before Brock could say anything else, worried about his brother's unprofessional behaviour. "Evelyn? Have you been brokering a deal on the side?"

"No, Sir, of course not. I am just as blindsided by this as you are!" she confirmed.

"And if Ms. Jones doesn't agree?" Charles asked.

"She will," Eric said confidently. "You take the afternoon to decide and call me tomorrow with your decision. Ms Jones had offered to show me how she safeguards against hacking, so I'm going to take her up on that, while she and I discuss her future."

"What? We don't have anything like that," Brock spat.

"You don't know half of what she has done for your company. You may take her for granted, but I won't." Eric winked at Brock, then turned to Evelyn. "Shall we?"

Torn.

Evelyn stood frozen. She didn't know what to do. Brock looked like he was about to blow his top off, one hundred percent giving her the "I'm going to fuck you up" eyes. While Eric stood there too casually, as if he didn't just potentially ruin her entire professional career.

I guess I could start a feet pic Only Fans account, she thought, as she contemplated what to do.

Her eyes were darting back and forth between Brock and Eric, when Charles caught her eye. He brought his hand up to rub his eyebrow, feigning distress. When her gaze landed on him, he mouthed the words "go," and gave her the slightest nod towards Eric. His eyes were apologetic. Evelyn didn't believe he knew the extent of the hold his brother had on her, but she knew he had to have suspected something was going on, and Brock's outburst had proven that.

Evelyn gave Charles a sly smile before packing up her belongings and escorting Eric back to her office.

"What the fuck was that?" Evelyn asked once the door to her office closed behind Eric.

"You're welcome?"

"You're welcome? Seriously? How about the next time you decide a major career move for me, you let me know first!" she fumed.

"Next time," he chuckled.

"Are you laughing? Do you not understand what you just did?" she asked, feeling hysterical.

"Yes, Evelyn, I got you out," he said calmly.

"I told you I had this handled," she reminded him.

The humour in Eric's features was replaced with desperation as he closed the distance between them, reached up and gently cupped her face.

"I believe you could have handled it yourself, but to think what you would have gone through while you waited fills me with this rage I had never felt before. I'm sorry I took this step without telling you, but I needed to do something. It was either this, or I was going to fucking kill the bastard with my bare hands. He is lucky I chose the less murderous route."

"What exactly am I being offered," she asked cautiously.

"You have options, your pick, really," he said, releasing her face, and gesturing for them to have a seat.

"Options?"

Eric spent the next hour presenting four different jobs and work locations, all on the other side of the country, away from the Collins' influence. Eric was getting her out, whether Charles accepted his contract terms or not.

They all sounded perfect.

Eric explained that all expenses for moving would be paid and she would have help with searching for an apartment, which is all standard when they poach their employees from other companies. This was a no-brainer for Evelyn. The only hard decision would be choosing which new city she wanted to live in.

"There is one more option," Eric said. He rubbed the back of his neck, unsure whether he wanted to tell her.

"I'm listening," Evelyn said, encouraging him to continue.

"There is an opening at our head office. Honestly, it's the best position being offered. With the other positions, you are one step away from management, but here, you would be in charge."

"Why do I feel like there is a 'but'"?

"Because there is," he sighed. "I'm just going to be straight with you. I like you. I know we have only known each other for a couple of days, but I would love to get to know you better. If you pick any of the first four positions, I feel like it would be okay, it wouldn't be inappropriate if I pursued something with you, but if you take the position at head office, at my office, it would be.

"Where I stand right now, your safety, well-being, and job security are my main priorities. I need to get you out. As far as I'm concerned, today is the last day you will see inside these office walls, and I have someone tailing Brock to make sure he stays away from you until you move. As much as I would love to date you, you should take the head office job. I honestly just want what's best for you."

"I need time to think."

"I assumed you would." Eric got up and opened the door to her office, and a large man walked in. He towered over Eric and had the physique of a bodybuilder. His dark hair was buzzed and he had tattoos crawling up his neck. He was a very intimidating man, but she noticed he had kind eyes.

"Evelyn, this is Hunter. He is going to stay with you while you pack up your office and escort you off the property. Please, don't go anywhere without him."

"Do you think a personal bodyguard is necessary?" she asked in disbelief.

The two men gave each other a knowing look before Hunter stepped back outside the door where he stood guard.

"I'm going to leave, so you can think without me influencing your decision."

Evelyn stepped around her desk and grabbed his arm.

"I'm going to see you again, right?" she asked.

"You will," he promised. He cupped the side of her face, stroking her cheek with his thumb. His eyes shined with what looked like regret, his brows furrowed, as his eyes took in her features, like he was studying her face, so he wouldn't forget it. "I'll call you in the morning for your answer."

He took her hand, kissed it, then left.

He assured her she would see him again, but he never said when.

CHAPTER ELEVEN

Everything was happening too fast.

She needed the world to stop spinning.

Evelyn thought it was ridiculous that Eric had assigned her a personal bodyguard. At first, she scoffed at the idea and even tried to send Hunter away after Eric left. But by the third time Hunter prevented Brock from entering her office, and intercepted his attempt to follow her into the washroom, she was grateful and relieved to have him there. He followed her home, and she suspected he would spend the night watching her apartment building.

When she got home, she didn't know what to do. She knew she was leaving. She had already packed up her office, and handed in all her I.D. badges.

Should she start packing her apartment?

Should she sit down and decide where she was going first?

What about Eric? Does she choose the better job, or choose him?

She had to make a decision. With so many options and factors to consider, she needed more time, but time was the only thing she didn't have.

Her brain broke. She sat motionless on the couch, paralyzed by indecision. It was too much.

The night crept up on her. She eventually poured herself a full glass of red wine and researched the cities she could potentially be moving to, including where his head office was located. The wine helped. In her relaxed, but slightly inebriated state, she was able to be more candid with herself, and easily eliminated three cities from the list. Why would she subject herself to harsh winters if she didn't have to?

The remaining locations were equal in desirability, but now she was back to debating between job, or Eric.

"Why didn't you get into the car with him that first day?" she angrily asked herself out loud. "Who gives a shit about your car. You played this wrong, you stupid bitch! You could have invited him up and had some fun. Now you may never see him again," she slurred.

She knew the answer, whether she chose to ignore it or not. He was different. There was something wholesome and good about him. He respected her and actually wanted to get to know her. Perhaps if she didn't get that vibe from him, she would have already sucked him off under a desk and then invited him back to her place to let him fuck whichever hole pleased him.

He cared and was selflessly putting aside what he wanted and how he felt for her greater good.

"Fuck, that's hot!" she moaned. "Focus..."

She needed to stop thinking with her pussy and make the best decision that would benefit her.

"Screw it, I'm going to sleep on it, see how I feel in the morning," she declared to her laptop.

She had a quick rinse in the shower and got ready for bed, hoping that the morning would bring more clarity.

Freaked out about the prospect of Brock getting into her building, despite her guard, she turned the light on in the kitchen on the way to her bedroom. She may have had ulterior motives for leaving it on.

Evelyn crawled into bed. Unable to help herself, she searched for Eric on her phone, looking at a few pictures, but she quickly passed out, the day's events finally catching up to her.

A warm, cold tingling sensation trailing along the side of her face, and down her neck woke her up. She opened her eyes and turned her head to face her muted midnight massager. He was lying beside her on his side, head propped up by one arm. He was looking down at her as he continued to run his fingers down her neck and across her collarbone and shoulder.

"You came back," she whispered.

He nodded yes while he wiped a tear rolling down her face. A flood of emotions overwhelmed her. She didn't realize how much she needed to see her naughty nocturnal nympho. She needed him to help her forget, and to just feel.

"Do you need me to sit up, so you can grab her?" Evelyn asked, gesturing to approximately where her shadow should be."

She moved to sit up, but he placed his hand on her shoulder to keep her down and shook his head no. He placed his hand on his chest, and then on hers, communicating what he desired.

"Just you and me tonight?" she clarified.

He nodded yes, and then tugged at her tank top strap.

Not needing to be asked twice, she grabbed her top by the hem and slowly pulled it up over her head, arching her back as she did so, to better display her breasts. He placed his palm flat on her stomach, and ran his hand up, continuing between her breasts, and to her neck, which he firmly grabbed. He tilted her head up and smashed his mouth onto hers. He used his grasp on her neck to angle her head to allow him to penetrate her mouth deeply, his tongue conquering every inch of her.

His hand released her neck and he brought it back down to her breasts. He slowly ran his hand over her, massaging, pinching, plucking, and squeezing, while he continued taking her mouth with his.

He grabbed Evelyn's hand, which she had curled into her sheets beside her, and placed it on her breasts. He encouraged her to play with herself while his hand made its way down to her already throbbing pussy. He grabbed her panties and ripped them off, not wasting any time on them, and then sunk two fingers into her wanting, wet cunt.

Realizing she was ready for him, he removed his fingers and stopped kissing her. She was ready and willing to be placed in whatever crazy position her sinful shadowy seducer wanted to put her in. Instead, he climbed on top of her and took her face to face.

She honestly couldn't remember the last time she had sex in the missionary position. Most guys she had been with felt like they had something to prove and took her every way but that.

There was that one time though, with the girl from the bar, and I wore a strap-on, she reminisced, but her thoughts were interrupted by a hard, fast thrust. It hit the right spot and she gasped. He pulled out and slammed into her again, hitting the same spot that had Evelyn seeing stars. At first, his thrusts were slow but impactful, but then he started speeding up the tempo until he settled on a fast, steady rhythm.

Holy hell, I'll never take this position for granted again, she thought.

"I'm...I'm going to come," she said breathlessly into his shoulder.

He kissed her quickly, then threw back his head as he silently orgasmed with her. She was not so quiet.

She melted into the mattress as her body recovered and she caught her breath. She expected her perverted penetrating perpetrator to collapse on top of her for the same reasons, but as it turned out, shadows don't need rest. He removed his cock, and slid down her body and immediately started to lick, suck, and nibble her pussy.

He spoiled her with three orgasms before she interrupted him. He would have kept going, but it was his turn to lie back. She wanted to play.

She ran her hands up and down his long, girthy shaft, enjoying the strange sensation of his shadowing skin. She teased him with her mouth, rubbed his cock all over her face, and jerked him off between her tits before she took his entire length down her throat. He grabbed onto her hair, and she let him still her head as he thrust up and fucked her mouth. She knew he came when he threw back his head, his telltale sign of his release.

Shadows didn't ejaculate. She wasn't sure if she was disappointed or relieved.

After another hour of her favourite positions, and learning a few new ones, which she didn't think was possible at this point in her life, a yawn escaped her lips. She tried to pass it off as a moan, but he caught it.

"I'm fine, don't stop," she pleaded, as he was taking her up against the wall with her legs wrapped around his waist.

He shook his head and carried her to the bed, where he laid her down and positioned himself on top to finish the night how it started. He was tender and sweet, as he kissed her and stroked her hair while keeping his thrusts at a stable speed. She imagined that if he had eyes, he would have been gazing affectionately into hers, eyes hooded, with nothing but appreciation shining through.

As they finished together he continued kissing her while he held her head, gently brushing his thumbs along her face. It was loving, protective, safe, and romantic. It also felt like a goodbye.

Her eyes flew open in realization, and she choked back a sob.

"I'm not going to see you again, am I?" she whispered.

He shook his head no. Although he had no features, she could read the regret in his body language.

"My life is such a mess, I don't know what to do. I know this sounds weird, but you are the only thing I am sure about right now," she chuckled in embarrassment.

He reached over to her nightstand, grabbed her phone, and held it up. She unlocked it with her finger, and the phone opened, showing the last picture of Eric she was looking at before she had fallen asleep. With his free hand, he touched the picture and then placed his hand on her heart.

"Yes, I like him, but it's not that easy," she admitted.

He hung his head down and placed the phone back on the nightstand. He placed his hand over her heart once more.

You'll know what feels right, a man's deep husky voice said inside her head.

She nodded, and took in a deep breath, letting it out slowly. He was right. She had to stop overthinking and just do what felt right.

"I don't want you to go. I...I'm not ready to say goodbye," she said softly.

He leaned in, and kissed her once more on the lips, then on her forehead. His fingers lingered on her face as his form dissolved, becoming a part of the surrounding darkness.

She expected tears because her heart was aching, but a part of her knew it was time to say goodbye. When she woke up in the morning she would be level-headed, her mind clear, and she would know her answer.

EPILOGUE

"Holy shit!" Evelyn dropped her fork, causing her eggs to splatter everywhere. "Did you see this?"

She held up her tablet to show the headline.

Brock Collins of Collins Industries found dead in his Apartment.

"That explains why my phone has been blowing up all morning," Eric said, his coffee cup hovering close to his mouth, too surprised to remember to take a sip. "I know this is our time together, but I better make a few calls. Do you mind?"

"No, of course not. I should probably be expecting my office to call shortly as well," she sighed.

Fucking Brock.

She was surprised by the news, but wasn't upset by it. Inconvenienced more than anything.

Eric bent to kiss her before he left to make his calls.

"Wait, Eric!" Evelyn called out before he could leave the room. He turned to face her expectantly. "Tell me the truth. Did you have anything to do with this?"

"No, this wasn't me," he assured her. "Why would I want him dead? I won. I got the girl and the deal of a century. How could I rub it in if he were dead?" He smirked and walked out of the room.

Evelyn watched Eric walk away, wondering if her teeth marks were still on his ass from the night before. When he walked out of view, she returned her attention to her tablet and read the article.

Brock Collins of Collins Industries found dead in his Apartment.

Local police found Brock Collins, 35 deceased in his apartment, late afternoon, Friday. His brother, and business partner, Charles Collins had called the local authorities for a welfare check after receiving a disturbing voicemail from Brock that morning and then failing to show up to work.

The police have not officially released a statement but it has been leaked that he was found in his living room naked, strangled by a belt.

There are no eyewitness accounts. Brock Collins lived in the penthouse apartment in the coveted Moonlight Towers downtown in Silver City.

Sources say that his apartment was locked from the inside, and his alarm system was armed. Security logs and elevator footage showed that Brock entered his penthouse apartment alone Saturday night, and the elevator wasn't granted access to it again that evening.

Many are speculating that this was a case of a self-pleasuring gone wrong.

. . .

BREAKING NEWS.

Brock Collin's voicemail message and 911 call have been leaked. Read the transcripts below.

Voicemail - Brock Collins to Charles Collins

*Heavy breathing

Charles, pick up. Motherfucker, if you are pulling some kind of prank...That's it, I'm changing my security codes. I'm walking to my living room right now, and if I find you passed out on my couch without calling again, I'm going to take a shit right on your...What the fuck!

*Call disconnected.

911 Call

Operator 911, what's your emergency?

Brock There's someone in my apartment.

Operator Okay, I can send the police. Where are you?

Brock Penthouse apartment, Moonlight Towers. This is Brock Collins.

Operator Ok Brock, help is on the way, are you safe?

Brock *heavy breathing

Operator Brock, what's happening?

Brock There's a man in my room.

Operator Where are you now?

Brock I'm hiding behind my couch in the living room. Oh God, What the fuck!

Operator Brock, talk to me.

Brock He just walked through the fucking wall. He just walked through the fucking wall!

No No No...
*screaming.
*Call disconnected.

Acknowledgments

Chats with friends are a dangerous thing.

Never, ever could I have imagined that I would write anything like this. My friend and I were joking about writing something completely out there. The Shadow Daddy tagline spewed out of my mouth, we had a good laugh and left it at that.

Eight days later, I had Shadowed Desires written.

Thanks to Tina, Tess Watters, and Sarah Cook for being amazing Beta readers. Your feedback and encouragement with this little project have been priceless and I appreciate you all so much!

Thank you to my readers for taking the chance and reading my fun novella project. I hope you were as entertained reading this as I was writing it.

Printed in Great Britain
by Amazon